VORN AND THE FIRST COMERS

KUSHLAN SILVERTONGUE : TALES FROM ARGENTERRA

DONNA MAREE HANSON

Copyright Information

First published by Australian Speculative Fiction (Donna Maree Hanson) in 2019.

Cover design by Patty Jansen www.pattyjansen.com

Proofread by Jason Nahrung

To report a typographical error, please email donnamareehanson@gmail.com

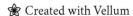 Created with Vellum

FOREWORD

Greetings to those who are reading this story of Vorn and the First Comers—a mighty tale of those brave folk who escaped violence and certain death and arrived in this world. I hope that the story will be pleasing to you, as it is the first in many tales that I am writing down to preserve them for future generations.

But first, a little about me. I am Cushion of the Valley but I am also known as Kushlan Silvertongue due to my life's work as a teller of tales. In truth, it is the Puri people who named me thus. My current work to write down these tales and preserve them is by the order of Oakheart, King of Argenterra. My daughter, Tu Raenal, a princess of Argenterra, has some influence there, you see, and I am now officially named Kushlan Silvertongue, Keeper of Tales.

My king has charged me to record as many tales

of Argenterra that I know already, and by his authority to seek out more by listening to the oral traditions of many families as well as researching facts and anecdotes in the great library at Glassy Mountain Retreat. I am supported in this by Hanal, Prince of Argenterra, who is also my son-in-law. Even without this commission, I would have striven to record all that I know because I believe the lives and deeds of the First Comers are important as their acts have made us who we are today. We owe everything to them.

My collection of tales will include other significant events that were passed down through the age as not only the acts of the First Comers, but the acts of all our forebears, affect us this day, just as what we do affects those who come after us. All my adult life I have told tales of our forebears, or my distant kin, and just those tales worthy of the telling. These I have orated in the mighty halls of kings, whispered over campfires in the land of Argenterra and recited in the tents of my Puri kin.

It has been my belief that such tales of the past enhance our lives, allow us to know our purpose and provide guidance so that we may learn from the mistakes of the past. For this reason, I commend these stories to you in the hope that they will bestow on you a smattering of wisdom as well as an enormous amount of pleasure. We cannot know the past in the way that our forebears lived it so these stories only give a glimpse, a bittersweet taste of what was and what might have been. Through these tales I hope to convey some sense of their world and their thoughts as honestly and as truly as I can.

In preparing this story for the collection commissioned by my king, I have compiled no fewer than twenty different versions of the story of Vorn and the First Comers' arrival in Argenterra. I have consulted a number of written accounts that are kept in the library at Glassy Mountain Retreat. Some of these writings were by Vorn himself and I have given due weight to them.

What follows is an account, which I think is most consistent with what we know of Vorn and his life before coming to Argenterra. I have disregarded some idiosyncratic variations of the story, which might aggrandise one family line over another. As you know most families trace their origin back to the First Comers and even claim to be descended from Vorn himself. Some of those claims could be disproved if such was my aim but as it is not, I will not be puncturing anyone's pride in their family's lineage. Not intentionally, at least.

Vorn led the First Comers to Argenterra and, thus, he belongs to all of us, direct descendant or no. I have endeavoured to be impartial. It is up to you, dear reader, to judge how well I have achieved this aim.

So it begins…

Picture if you will Yulandir, the world from whence Vorn and his brethren came—a barren, broken world, with the smoke of many fires curling up to a darkened sky. The dead and the dying were many, left where they dropped. Cities once vast were but spines of metal reaching through the dead soil, like hands grasping for one last chance of life. There was nothing left, except the aftershock of unspeakable weapons and the stench of putrefaction.

I speak not of what caused the war that destroyed their home world, only of their need and desire for flight. The tale of Vorn and the Ancient Evil belongs as a tale of its own and I look forward to presenting it to you in my collection of Argenterran tales, but for now I will give you this account of Vorn and the First Comers as they prepared to flee.

CHAPTER 1

ESCAPE FROM YULANDIR

*Y*ulandir could no longer sustain life—its air tainted with poisons and smoke from the weapons sent from above. Vorn knew the battle was done. Only the remnants of his kin remained alive and thoughts of battle had to turn to survival.

Standing on the once fertile plain, Vorn surveyed the destruction, his heart wracked with guilt, fist clenching his now useless sword. Could he have prevented this? Vorn was certain he could have somewhere in the past months, before he had been sucked into this vortex of chaos and carnage. Surely, the blame was his. The losses were incalculable. Behind him, the city of Halfa was a smoking ruin of broken buildings and smashed roads and bridges. Nothing living stirred there. The scent of death crawled out to where he stood in the dust to accuse him.

The survivors, numbering less than fifty, gathered around him. He stood head and shoulders above them, his blond hair caked in dirt and sweat and blood, his sword clenched in his hand with its power waning. There was nothing left to do but flee.

Some of the survivors carried possessions. Others barely kept their clothes on their backs. The sky boomed ominously. A bomb? A power generator exploding? A sky ship falling? He knew not. The smoky, hot air was hard to breathe. They had to leave. Now.

"It is time," he said to those around him.

"Time for what, brother?" Shabra said. His younger brother was shorter and darker than Vorn and he had suffered during the brief war. His arm showed burn scars and his face was nicked and bloody from fighting hand-to-hand. The war had tainted Shabra's spirit and Vorn tried his best to be patient with him.

"Escape," Vorn replied.

"Escape to where? There is nowhere left to go. We may as well lie down and die now. Or offer ourselves to her and hope she likes salvage."

Vorn clasped his brother on the shoulder. "There is a way to leave this planet. A doorway between worlds. I have seen her summon it."

"You want to use her technology?" Shabra spat,

his lips curling in horror. He drew away, eyes loaded with pain and distrust.

"Yes. It's the only way any of us will get out of here. I know how to use it. But we must move now." He scanned the group of refugees. "Is this all of you? Are there no more to be found?"

People shook their heads. "No one that I could see," called a young man.

A sob. "They are dead!" This from an old woman.

Vorn's heart clenched with sorrow but there was no time for grief. Not now. Maybe later. If they survived long enough.

He stepped to where he had seen the magnificent crystal gate appear a year ago. When he had seen the beautiful Unesta step through into Yulandir. Then it had been a vibrant world, rich in resources and life. He pushed that memory aside and spoke the words of summoning, ones he had overheard and memorised. Immediately, he detected the thrum of power. He knew when it became visible from the cries of wonder and surprise behind him.

"Be careful," Shabra said and grabbed his forearm. "I do not trust this...this thing."

Vorn met his gaze unflinchingly, faces close together. "What choice do we have? To stay means certain death. With this there is a chance of survival."

Shabra released his hold, his face clenched with distrust, shaking his head slowly.

The gate fully materialised, sending out shafts of

bright light, blue, yellow, white. Vorn sheltered his eyes with his hand. "Come," he called. "Step through."

No one moved. "Shabra?"

His brother shook his head.

"Will not someone go first? I must stay until you are all through to close it. There is no point fleeing if they can follow after us."

An old woman shuffled forward, holding her side where a wound bled. "I will go first."

Vorn smiled at her. "I thank you. What is your name?"

"My name is Faruni. I have spent fifty years in this life and I am not willing to die yet."

"May you live fifty more. Go through and wait just beyond. There is a corridor there where we will join you."

She nodded and, straightening her spine and lowering her chin, walked forward. The light soon swallowed her.

Smoke wafted over them and the refugees began to cough.

"Next," Vorn called. A young man strode forward, acknowledged Vorn with a nod and followed Faruni. That broke the hesitation. Now people were pushing to go through, holding onto each other as visibility ebbed. Shabra stood with his mouth covered by his hand and shook his head. His eyes were red and tears ran down his dirty cheeks from the smoke.

People pushed past him and disappeared from view.

"Come, brother," Vorn said, arm outstretched and beckoning.

Shabra lifted his dark eyes to Vorn, wiped the moisture from his cheeks and gave him a nod. Shoulders hunched, he stepped into the light, into the portal behind a group of three women.

A surprised cry echoed and then cut off. Vorn assumed a fighting stance, eyes assessing the crowd. There at the rear he saw movement. Squinting at first, his eyes widened when he realised three of the enemy hacked at a fallen man. Surely, they had killed enough.

"Hurry," he said to those nearest him. "Keep moving." Then he pushed his way through to protect those at the rear.

An attacker loomed out of the smoke. Vorn lifted his sword to meet the challenge and deflected the deadly blow. Blades clashed and power rippled. His sword had energy yet. Two others came at him. In his peripheral vision, he saw two young men hesitate. With a shove against his attacker, he called out, "Run! Go!"

The youths ran. The two attackers had superior weapons and the power in Vorn's sword was low, but it had a sharp edge yet. He parried two blows and back stepped. A device around the neck of one of his attackers was aimed at him. There was a bang and it was as if he had been punched in the chest. The blow sent him back, end over end. He dropped his weapon in the dirt. Momentarily stunned, it took him a few seconds to get to his feet.

With the gate behind him, he knew he was so close to freedom. He could not let himself end like this. Staggering and disoriented, he did not move fast enough when one of them came at him. He had only his hands and he used them, smashing out at his assailants with heavy fists. He back stepped again. He was close to the crystal gate. He had no time to search for other survivors and those that had gathered there had passed through.

The weapon hit again, some kind of beam, barely noticeable, but the effects drained him, made his limbs feel like deadweight, his eyelids heavy as steel. He dropped to the ground and the remainder of the beam passed over him. He recovered quickly, except his shoulder was numbed from the touch of the weapon. It was no time for nice tactics. He clenched dirt in his hand—grey, lifeless soil that once held rich crops—and flung it in a wide circle. His attackers cried in surprise. Vorn took his chance and lurched straight for the gate, his empty scabbard hitting against his thighs.

A child had fallen before him and he leaned down to scoop him up, flinging the small body ahead into the opening.

Vorn spoke the code words that would seal the

gate behind him. It closed with a snap and a rush of air that propelled him to the ground.

Vorn lay on the cool floor. It wasn't earth but some other substance that was rock that appeared to be as smooth as metal. He opened his eyes to a corridor of light. He knew enough to not be afraid but naught else. Climbing to his feet, he saw the corridor was full of people. Too many people. Some were obviously not his refugees. Yet they looked to him with a hunger in their eyes and signs of violence on their persons. This was a pathway between worlds, so he should not be surprised to find people from elsewhere within.

Voices called to him asking for direction.

"Move ahead. Move forward."

All seemed to understand him, and he edged his way through the bodies blocking his path so that he could find the head of the column. Surely there were another fifty people at least, he thought, as he squeezed past men, women and children.

Shabra glowered at him as he came up. "What kept you?" his brother asked, his body hunched as he tried not to touch the fabric of the corridor, which was shimmering and translucent. Vorn eyed it, too. It looked too flimsy to contain them.

"It does not matter now. We are safe."

"You are bleeding." Shabra said as he looked him up and down. "Your sword?"

Vorn shook his head. "We were attacked." Vorn

surveyed his surroundings. "We must exit soon. They might find us if we are still within the gate."

"How do you know where to leave this place? I can see nothing. Just this endless corridor of light."

"It is a tunnel, a pathway between worlds. Do not ask me to explain it. I know not if it is a construct or a natural phenomenon."

Shabra's eyes widened but he did not speak again. How could one respond to such a marvel? Vorn had been speechless when he first learned of it. Vorn stepped up to where he thought the doorway would be. He spoke the code. Nothing happened.

He walked further along and checked over his shoulder. He had a crowd of onlookers trying to peer over the person in front to see. Turning away, Vorn shut them out, the noise, their presence, their worries. This was not about humiliation and not being able to command the doorway, it was about survival. They needed to find a place to live and live in peace.

He closed his eyes, trying to get some sense of this pathway between worlds. Something beyond sight beckoned to him. It was uncanny, not something he had experienced before—an ethereal thread that tugged at other senses, senses he barely knew he had. Senses he did not understand or command.

But like his people, he had been changed by events. He knew not what he was anymore. He had been tortured, experimented on with alien technology, exposed to magics and tactics that were beyond his experience and comprehension. How much of him was the man who had been Vorn? It did not matter. He was who he was and this place that called to him, this place that reached out with a feather-like touch...he had to seize it and save his people.

He called out the code again and the door opened. This time bright light near blinded him. He covered his eyes and peered out. Through the open door cool air rushed in.

CHAPTER 2

THE FIRST GLIMPSE

"*C*ome out, come out!" he called and stepped through. "Follow me to safety."

The air was fresh and laced with ice. He breathed deeply, clearing his lungs of dust and smoke and the stench of death. Cries and exclamations reached his ears as he continued away from the gate to make room for those who followed.

Gazing up, he saw a corrugated mountain range against the blue of the sky, and then, turning, he beheld the land, green and lush, spreading out as far as his eyes could see. A valley shrouded in mist, forests extending to the sea to the south of them, and a lake that reflected silver in the sun sitting right in the centre. The sun rose higher and the land shimmered like a glittering shield. It was a silver land.

Something else brushed against his heightened senses. There was power here, power he could sense and taste and perhaps use, if he had the will. As the people flowed out of the crystal gate, Vorn quieted his mind and meditated.

He shut out the sounds of voices and cries and moans and people talking that swirled around him. He caught a trickle of something. Power. Awareness. Perhaps they were combined. He breathed out, delved deeper into himself, into his connection to whatever it was. Unesta's experimentation had changed him. He had thought that it was for the worse, but now he realised it was for the better. She had opened up his mind to something unseen, something greater than he was. He thought Unesta would not like this result. She hated anything that challenged her superiority.

Then he found it. His blood pumped hard and his breath drew in harshly. Vast power. This silver land had power.

Shabra called his name and shook him by the shoulder. "Brother? What are you doing standing there like an idiot?"

Vorn opened his eyes, spun slowly about and smiled at his half-brother. He stood head and shoulders above the others. He had been a mighty warrior. He had fought the battle and lost. Now it was time to turn his mind to peace and protection. These people had followed him through the gate and now he needed to provide for them and give them direction.

The crystal gate stood unmoving with its bright light bathing them in a bluish glow. He nodded to the people who were looking to him. Others were taking in their surroundings. There was no smoke here. No war.

"Is everybody through?" he asked, squinting against the light.

"Yes!" someone called. "No more follow."

Vorn strode to the gate and uttered the code. The light brightened and he shielded his eyes and then it was gone, leaving nothing but dark patches in his eyes. He blinked a few times and turned back to his people, his vision clearing.

He caught sight of a small tree. It was leafless and could have been mistaken for dead. Yet he sensed within it a deep magic, a magic within this land. Another glance around him at the refugees and then he studied the tree. They were hungry, had hardly any provisions with them. They needed something, a sign, maybe something more concrete like food to let them know that they were now safe.

Vorn strode down a stone pathway toward the tree. It was a natural path, not made by human hands. The crystal gate had brought them to this place and it was empty of people. He was certain of that. For as far as his eye could see this place had no owner, other than the power that pulsed beneath his feet. With that power he needed to negotiate.

The tree was strange to his eye, dull-grey and

spindly. The wind rocked its bare branches. Yet, he could see more in it. As his hand neared, power throbbed and his fingertips tingled in reaction. He stroked a bare branch. He was not imagining it. Closing his eyes, he reached out again with his other sense.

"Tree," he said aloud. "Tree, give us your bounty for we hunger."

The power grew hot under his fingertips. He had no idea anything had changed until he heard the cries of surprise. Behind him, the refugees had gathered. He opened his eyes. A leaf had sprouted on the tree. It was no ordinary leave but appeared to be star shaped, round with spikes on the outside. More of the leaves sprouted, and then golden fruit emerged. The aroma was pleasing and his tongue watered.

"Thank you," he said to the tree and plucked the nearest fruit. He broke it open and ate some of the yellow flesh. It was sweet and creamy and he swallowed it.

"It could be poison," Shabra said, making a grab for the food.

"It is not. But I eat of it first so that you will trust in it. This land has given us its bounty."

Shabra gaped. His stare was part horror, part suspicion. "How?" Shabra rasped out.

"I asked and it was given."

"Given?" Shabra said like he was gulping the word. His forehead creased in puzzlement. The word was taken up by the people who gathered around to pluck the fruit. They did not wait to see if Vorn had ill effects. As they ate their fill, Vorn closed his eyes, listening to the will of the land. That was the only description he could use to describe it.

He opened his eyes and saw the people. Some were kin and friends. Others were strangers already within the pathway between the worlds when he entered. All bore signs of violence, from mere haunted looks to bloody injuries. Vorn himself was scarred within from the violence, from the total annihilation of Yulandir.

There was much to do. They needed to move from this mountain to the fertile valley below and he had to find a way to bar Unesta from this land. The land with its silver lake and its silver-barked tree was a silver land. He would name it Argenterra.

It came to him then what must be done—a way to bind the magic of this land to the people. A pledge was needed to keep these refugees from harm. The land would protect them in exchange for an oath.

"Gather around," he called to those around him. "Come closer. I have something to say."

His people heard him and gathered close in a semi-circle. His brother Shabra scowled but stood close, his gaze shifting from the people to Vorn.

"Listen," Vorn began. "The crystal gate has brought us to a haven and we have a chance to make a new start. Most of you fled the deadlands of

Yulandir with me." He hesitated when his eyes fell upon the dark-skinned ones. Had they fled with them or were they already within the gate, searching for a way out? They looked as raw-boned and used as the rest. Again he spoke. "You know what forced us to flee. We lived by violence, only to die by it. We must forsake bloodshed, aggression and harm in this place to survive. If we vow to do this, the Ancient Evil cannot pursue us to this place. This land, its magic will protect us and her hand will not be able to reach here and sully this world. This land will make a pact with us if we will return one in kind."

There was a rumble of voices in the crowd. Shabra came forward as if struggling for words. Finally, he spluttered. "Are you mad?"

They locked gazes. "No. I am not mad but I am not who I was before this tragedy began." He turned to the rest of the people. "We have to deny violence. This land will provide protection if we do."

The old woman who had been first through the gate hobbled forward, her eyes blue and bright as she spared Shabra a glance of irritation. "I am Faruni. Vorn has led us through the gate. He is worth ten of you. I will hear what he has to say." She turned to Vorn. "What you ask is noble but very difficult. How do we leave the taint of ages, the violence that is inborn, behind? Words are easily destroyed by deeds."

"I admit it is a difficult decision," he replied to her

and then lifted his voice so all could hear. "And it will be hard at first. But I have sensed a power here, a benevolent one. It gave us this fruit to fill our bellies. Out there is a wide, green land that will give us what we need to live a good life. This is our one real chance for a future. Think of our descendants. They will inherit this paradise from us if we do this. If we do not do this, then we will die. There will be no future. Not here, not anywhere."

"Did you say the land had power? It's nothing but earth and rock." Shabra glowered and wiped at the blood still leaking from the wound on his forehead.

Faruni elbowed Shabra in the ribs, startling him. "I would hear how we are to bind this power to us. Did you not see the fruit appear on that barren tree? Do you have so little faith?"

Shabra scowled at her. "I was not asking you, old woman."

"I may be old, young man, but I'm not a craven such as you. Where is your courage?"

Shabra scowled at her and hissed under his breath.

Certain of what the power had whispered to him, Vorn nodded and smiled encouragingly to those gathered. "We will make an oath—a binding oath. The land will seal it with its power." That they would be powerless to break their oath once they had made it he did not say. He only suspected this to be the case but for now he wanted to obtain their agreement. Let them discover the repercussions later.

If they would not vow then they would have to return through the crystal gate and go elsewhere. This was not the only world that the gate visited. Of that he was certain. But his heart told him this was the best place for them. No other people lived here. They could live free and in a society without violence. They could make their own life.

Old women, the men and the ragged, hollow-eyed children stared at him, mouths gaping and expressions incredulous. Even the old woman, Faruni, who seemed to have so much faith in him, looked doubtful.

Shabra's snarling face expressed all his disbelief. Vorn's hope plummeted. Did they all feel like his kinsman who was so ready to reject hope? He wanted to spit.

Staring at the ground, he decided to kneel. He would make the oath regardless of whether they followed his initiative.

Ignoring the cuts and nicks on his legs that bled into the dirt, he knelt on the ground and removed his empty scabbard, placing it on the ground beside him. A drop of blood tickled his chin before it, too, fell and mixed with the rest. He felt power building —the power of his blood coming to seal his oath.

He cleared his throat and spoke loudly so all

could hear. "I give my oath to this land, which I call Argenterra, the Silverland. I will serve it, treasure it and do no ill to it, its bounty or its people. I forswear violence and call on Argenterra to witness my oath. All those who bear my blood will be bound by my words and so it will continue through the ages."

Vorn felt at peace as his voice echoed around him. His gaze sifted through the refugees. One by one they copied his example and fell to their knees and repeated his oath word for word. All of their descendants would be bound just as his would be.

Only Shabra stood, snarl at his lips, looking down on them. He caught Vorn's look and held it. Something passed between them. Shabra's stormy gaze changed, his face softened and lost its hard lines. Then nodding he went to his knees and repeated the oath.

When the sound of Shabra's words died, the ground rumbled. The women wailed and the men cried out until their voices were cut off by gasps of wonder. They climbed to their feet and gaped at the land around them. Water bubbled from the ground in front of Vorn, then spouted into a fountain. Vorn was the first to lean forward and suck the cool, sweet water into his mouth. With a smile, he encouraged the rest of them to drink. One by one, they came forward to quench their thirst. Their complaisance brought new vigour to his plans for the future.

These people trusted him. He would lead them down into the valley to make their new lives. Now that he had made his vow, power came when beckoned. He was not a skilled user of this power and he worked mostly by instinct. He needed to bar the way into this world so that Unesta could not follow.

"Shabra?"

"Yes," his brother replied.

"Take these people away from here. I must bar the way so that the Unesta cannot enter."

"Where do you want me to take them?" Shabra asked.

"Just there," he pointed and Shabra followed his direction. "See, there is a path there. Wait for me below. I must do this first and then I will take you to the valley."

Shabra nodded. "What about that?" He nodded in the direction of the water. Some were still drinking.

"It will reabsorb when they are done."

Shabra shook his head. "How do you know this? I feel nothing of this power. Nothing of this oath. It's all just in your imagination."

Vorn chuckled. "Really? So you just drank imaginary water? Is this a group hallucination or a personal one just for you?"

Shabra grunted and bared his teeth. "Why you? What makes you so special?"

"I am changed." Vorn frowned as the memories of

what he had endured and what he had done came crowding back into his mind. He fought those visions off.

"You can say that again."

Vorn stepped closer to his brother. "In essence I am what I was. The experiments have changed me, yes. I can feel this power. You have seen it and you must believe it."

Shabra nodded. "I will do as you ask. Can you prevent her coming after you?"

"I believe I can."

Shabra called to the people to follow him and Vorn approached the place where the gate had deposited them. He knew the codes that summoned it. He needed to now blend this technology with the land's magic. He summoned the gate again and walked around the space. He saw that it was only partly in this world, a projection into it. As he studied it, the thought came to him that he could ask the land, Argenterra, to bar the way to Unesta. He nodded and rubbed his chin, thinking of how to word this barrier so that the magic would work against this being who would chase him, just to kill those who followed him.

He studied the gate some more, seeing a use for it. They would need supplies and maybe animals for eating and for work. He could travel to the other worlds and fetch these, so it was important that the gate remained functional. Yet, he also did not wish it to be at anyone's beck and call. He stepped into the gate and the light surrounded him. He had the codes of summoning and dismissal. He went through those codes he had stolen and memorised. There was a setting for repeat so that the gate would go through a cycle, appearing now and then in the different worlds. This was the best solution. He used this code and stepped back out into Argenterra. The gate flashed a brilliant light and the ground shook and then it was gone. On the ground where the gate had once stood was a raised dais of stone, smooth as if it had been polished. Surrounding it was just normal stone. It was visible up close but not obvious from a distance.

He studied the peaks around him and thought this place would make a nice retreat one day, a place of study and repose with a good position from which to guard the gate.

Silently thanking the crystal gate for its service, although it was not a sentient being, but a device, he went to join his people. All around him, he could feel the land's power. It appeared to grow with each step he took. He wondered at that. Was that coming from him or had it been there already and was attracted to him somehow?

The people ahead of him on the path let him pass and some reached out to touch his shoulder, his forearm, his hand and give him thanks. Vorn cringed inwardly as he saw the look of adoration in their eyes. It made him uncomfortable for he was unworthy of their adulation. He worked to ameliorate a wrong that could not be undone and the guilt sat heavily on him.

CHAPTER 3

SETTLING IN

*I*t took two full days to get down the mountain proper, even with the assistance of the rocky path they followed. At least they did not have to climb down a cliff face or anything else as dire. Vorn shuddered at the thought. Without equipment and with various injuries they would have been stuck. Several times Vorn called on the land to provide water and food. Water was easy, food less so. Yet green shoots emerged from the rocks and, although bitter in taste, they were filling.

Once down into the valley, there was food aplenty. The ground of the lush green pastures felt soft and warm after the rock of the mountain they had slept on. Water came at anyone's bidding, not just Vorn's. And trees bore fruit at the bidding of the men, the women and the few children that came with them. Vorn could almost taste the change in his people. Gone was the despair and in its place, hope and joy and wonder. All shared in the land's power. For the first time in a long time, Vorn knew he had done the right thing.

As a group they continued on to the shelter of the woods. Vorn smiled and his heart filled with a contentment he had never thought he would experience. As the days went by, the people grew more confident in their surroundings. No longer were they dependent on him and they came to understand the gift their vow had bestowed on them. They could command the land's magic. All of them. Each one. Even Shabra the doubter could call water.

Four-legged beasts ran wild. These they called velders. One was brought down for eating. Shabra and others had their knives with them and rudely fashioned spears. The plains held wild grain and green-leafed vegetables. When they dug in the ground they found tubers that when cooked were bland but filling.

That first night in the valley, a detail of men and women collected wood and made a fire stack and the people gathered around it. With full bellies, they could make plans. But there was a problem.

"How will we make fire?" Shabra asked him. "We have no flame, no tinder."

Vorn walked around the pile of wood that was as high as his waist. It was the same height as the woman Faruni. Vorn thought on this problem well into the afternoon. The sun's rays were fading the sky to pale violet and dimness crept from the trees surrounding the clearing where people sat.

Vorn walked toward the stacked wood and reached out his hand. Just as the trees gave their fruit so too did the wood their fire. Flame and warmth bathed him. As he looked on, he saw that the wood was not burning. It was giving off heat and light but was not being consumed by the act. Once again, the land had met their need.

It took a while for the onlookers to notice. Shabra glared at the fire, the red flames reflecting off his scowl. So it was with Shabra. Every wonder stoked his anger rather than his wonder. Vorn did not think he could cure that, although he would try. Shabra was kin, a brother. They shared a mother.

As they gathered warmth from the fire and cooked the meat, Vorn tried not to think on his losses—a mother who was dead, along with all his extended family. He doubted his sleep would ever be free of the terrors of the war and the days preceding it.

He had only the scabbard now. His sword was lost. His sword of power, stolen from those who would conquer them.

A young woman with long dark hair approached him. She had a platter woven from large leaves bearing roasted meat and vegetables. "Will you take some food?" she asked in a quiet voice.

Her skin was pale as moonlight and Vorn smiled and thanked her. "What is your name?" Vorn asked.

"N'Brell, Lord Vorn."

Vorn chuckled at the honorific. "Just Vorn. I am no lord."

She smiled and shook her head. "You are our lord. Some say you should be our king."

"Hardly. We are but few. There is no need for a king."

She knelt in the grass beside him and looked into his face, the light dancing in her eyes. "Now we are few, but we will grow and there will be many of us in this great, fertile land. Trust in the future."

He studied her then nodded before picking up a portion of meat. "Thank you for the food and the words of wisdom."

She rocked back onto her heels and rose from her kneeling position and then she walked away to join her friends. Her words comforted him. He had to think more positively about the future.

When the food was done, those that wanted to talk gathered around him. The night was dry and mild but the fire's warmth was welcome. Vorn thanked Argenterra for its bounty and for the *given* magic. *Given*…that was what the magic should be called. He would tell the others of this great thought. The name *Given* would always remind people that the land has provided the magic in exchange for their vow.

There was much to do, though. They needed to build houses, develop industry and explore the land to see what other resources it held. That journey of discovery was before them. The immediate need was to build shelters and ensure they had enough stores. This land grew cold in winter and Vorn guessed that they were in the spring. There was not much that they carried with them. Vorn was at a loss to know how to address this. Perhaps in future he could venture back through the gate to find materials in other worlds and bring them here. Such a thing was not to be thought of now as his people needed him. What if he encountered Unesta within the ways between worlds? It was too soon. She would not give up? Not yet. Perhaps never.

He sat brooding as darkness grew around them. A cough sounded and another and he realised that the people were waiting for him to speak. He looked at them in turn.

"What should our priorities be?" he asked.

"Shelter," was the first response.

"We have been lucky and there has been no rain. A green land such as this must get lots of rain. We may find ourselves wet."

"What equipment do we have?" Vorn asked. "We should do a stock take. See what we have, what we need and what we can fashion. What about temporary accommodation?"

"Do you mean tents?" Shabra asked.

"Yes, tents or lean-tos of some kind. A simple structure that could provide shelter."

There were nods.

"I can construct some simple shelters with minimal tools," said another man, who had a heavy beard. There had been no time for baths or shaving.

"Then tomorrow we should start on those," Vorn said.

"There are plants around here that we could use for making fabric," Faruni said. N'Brell, sitting next to her, nodded.

"We could experiment," a sturdy middle-aged man said. "If we have some sharp tools, we could design a loom so we could make fabric. It will not be quick."

Vorn smiled. "That is an excellent idea. In time we will need clothes and blankets, and adapting to this place and making what we need is a good start." Vorn's heart warmed at the thought of the future. This talk of industry made the future of Argenterra more real. They could survive. The land was on their side and their people had skills.

They talked long into the night and then they slept under the stars. Vorn lay there looking up, noticing there was a second moon following the larger one. The stars were different from the constellations that graced Yulandir's skies. He would never see his home again. No, he thought. Home was a deadland now. It was gone—a memory, full of sadness and shame. He thought of Unesta and the early days of their acquaintance. If he had known then what would happen, would he have acted differently?

He tried not to think about it. He had the rest of his life to feel guilt. He closed his eyes and straight away the sounds of battle were in his ears and the smell of death and smoke in his nostrils. He hoped those who slept near him did not hear his whimpers.

Strong sunlight pierced his eyelids and he had to wake. Noises of those around him filled the air. Already the camp was in motion. Food was cooking. Children ran about. He had thought there was but a few but there was at least ten. On second look he realised that two of them he had mistaken for adults.

He walked through the camp and accepted a leaf full of some kind of mashed root vegetable. "What is this?" he asked after taking a bite.

"We are calling it toffel. Tasty, don't you think?"

He took another bite. "Yes, filling, too."

Later, he asked to be shown the toffel plants and he saw they were everywhere and that it would make a good staple. As well, the bland root they had found took on flavours of things cooked with it. His heart swelled with thanks. Surely, they were in paradise.

Over the next week, there were only a few complaints. Some storage huts were built and families had shelter in lean-tos. Work had begun on the looms and N'Brell, Faruni and another woman, Leeta, had made a good start on harvesting plants and spinning thread. He watched them during a whole afternoon and even participated, with Leeta and N'Brell showing him how to spin the fine threads. Tried to, at least. His fingers were not nimble, used as they were to sword fighting.

The children were sent in search of plants and bark that could be used for dye.

The stock take of tools and other possessions was sobering. There was not much. A number of knives, which had been used to cut branches for the lean-tos and kill velders. It was clear that they needed to find ore to make more tools to help with construction and tilling the soil. Only two people had the requisite skills. Although he hated to send them off on their own, he dispatched Welli and Tomas to look for signs of ore. They took off to follow the river back toward the mountains, taking some supplies with them. They were confident that the land's bounty would provide for them.

Vorn decided to cease worrying. If those two found a source then all would be well. He travelled around the camp, visiting the different folk. Here he came upon those who had already been in the ways between the worlds inside the gate.

The leader of this group was a woman called Lilt. She was mature and had two daughters. Her people were swarthy and dressed differently to Vorn's, in coloured robes and headdresses. "Greetings," Vorn said. "I would talk to you of where you come from and why you were within the gate."

Lilt stood up, her posture stiff with affront. "Why do you want to know? We are all here now with no means of return."

He lifted his hands to placate her. "Only interest. The workings of the crystal gate is of interest to me. I thought it was only the refugees fleeing my world that were within."

"Are we not welcome then?" she asked.

"Of course you are. None have said otherwise, I hope."

He lifted his eyebrow in query and she shook her head. "No, none have spoken to us."

Vorn was puzzled by this and realised that this woman spoke his tongue. "Are you from Yulandir?"

"No, we are not."

"You speak our tongue well."

She frowned at this. "I thought you were speaking our tongue."

Vorn laughed. "The magic of this place is a wonder. Be welcome in Argenterra. We hope to build homes for everyone in due course."

She bowed low. "We thank you. We do not need constructions. I beg leave though to work with those women who are making cloth. We would like to make tents and clothing. This is an important industry for us."

"Is there anything else you require?" Vorn asked.

"Our people have helped in the harvesting of the toffel plant. This we like as well as other things. We are willing to share what we know about identifying plants for eating. Misha here is good at identifying edible fungus."

"All you are willing to share is valuable and we are grateful."

He walked away, leaving Lilt to her people. The woman was sly, he thought, or maybe distrustful was a better description. He tried not to let that prejudice him against her and her people. She was only after what was best for them. Vorn wanted what was best for them all.

Vorn helped build shelters with the others. It was a useful skill and one that wasn't too difficult. He had been a warrior and an administrator. Some useful work was good for the soul. Besides, the refuges appeared to appreciate his efforts and he had some measure of pride in creating things.

Again, the fire was built up with wood. This time another person called forth the flame and Vorn watched as the wonder and joy filled the faces of those who watched and also the man who used the *given*. Tonight, he would tell them the name he had labelled the magic.

The aroma of food made his belly rumble as he made his way to where it was being served. Again N'Brell passed him a plate. "This time we have found honey and baked the toffel with it. A delicious meal indeed."

Vorn inhaled it and then tasted a portion pinched from the plate between finger and thumb. It was heavenly—smooth, sweet and so rich. "That is truly amazing. Thank the land for all that it has given us."

"Yes, thank Argenterra. Thank you for allowing this to be."

He smiled and shook his woven plate off, his mind contemplating N'Brell's words. They truly thought their present bounty was due to him. It was he who had sensed the magic and what it required. But would not another have done the same? He did not know. Shabra, he thought, was too angry, too out of touch with the world around him, to have done so. Maybe N'Brell was correct.

Vorn tried to keep modest about this and, also, tried not to believe the praise lavished on him. His guilt at the destruction of his home world kept him grounded. Argenterra was a second chance for him, for all of them. He had to make it work.

One day, not more than a couple of weeks into the settlement, Vorn strode through the wood and ventured into the forest beyond. He needed to contemplate his many faults. There was much to ponder of the past, the present and the future. The past was uncomfortable to consider but so much could be learned from mistakes. His and others. Especially his. The present was full of activity. So much to do and he had yet to settle on a task for himself. He had assisted but not decided on a skill for himself. He oversaw and encouraged others but that would not be enough in the long term.

Fallen branches crackled underfoot and light broke through the treetops in bright shafts, looking like prisms. He paused to look around him. No other had trodden this path before. This world was fresh and new. He frowned. Was Argenterra truly untouched? He made a mental note to explore this question. He had assumed so as there appeared no trace of current or previous occupants. Then surely Argenterra was only part of a greater world. How far would the magic extend? What were the boundaries of Argenterra?

Cool, moist air filled his lungs as he continued his journey into the deeper forest. They would need wood to build houses and he wondered about the impact of that. This land was so beautiful it would be a pity to mar it, nay, a crime. He would see if there were other ways to build that did not consume the wonders of the world.

A stream gurgled nearby and he turned toward it. He could sense the water beneath the ground, too, waiting to be summoned by the *given* magic. Oh what a wonder. The wide stream was fast flowing. When he put his hand into the water, he knew it to be cold and fresh from the snow melt from the mountains above. He took a seat under a tree and contemplated the scene.

As Vorn's mind relaxed thoughts came: small concerns, larger worries and speculation on the future. What would become of his people? *His* people? He called them that because that was what they were to him now. All of them regardless of where they came from. All eyes looked to him and they listened to his counsel. It was a huge responsibility. If only they knew what a fraud he was, what he was responsible for. He let that guilt lie and contemplated on the future and what this world would bring. His people would grow dependent on the *given*. It made sense. Already they called on it and soon the magic would be so much a part of their lives that they would use it instinctively. He thought on the children who would be born in Argenterra and how the *given* would be natural to them, something that was part of their lives and no longer a marvel.

There was a risk, though, to this dependence. What if the magic disappeared? He sat there on his own, caught in his own dark thoughts until night came and cool dew settled on his skin. Lost to time and deep in thought, he continued to sit there contemplating. At some point, he fell asleep. But it was no ordinary sleep...

CHAPTER 4

VISIONS

I beg to intrude here, dear readers. There are several accounts of Vorn's visions in existence and a strong oral tradition concerning them. I have relied on Vorn's own account and on N'Brell's. She wrote of them in her journal. Both writings were recorded several weeks and, perhaps, years after the event and might be expected to have some filtering and post-vision analysis contained within. I have disregarded other accounts such as Shabra's accounting and that of the Grayhouse line, which contained some farfetched predictions and derogatory narrative about Vorn. These discarded accounts varied significantly from Vorn's own account, which was written in his own hand and is now housed at Glassy Mountain Retreat and must be held as a truer resource. Next time you visit Glassy Mountain Retreat be sure to ask the adepts for permission to view Vorn's writings. A truly remarkable experience, I assure you. Now back to Vorn...

Visions assailed Vorn—visions that scared him deep in his soul. The evil they had fled followed them to this place and reached in a hand. He saw the magic drain away. With a sense of awe, he beheld images of future towns and grand buildings. He saw his people prosper and his sense of pride grew. Then, looking wider across the land, he detected inequality and the resulting discord this created. Sadness grew in his heart. From here, the visions grew in darkness and took on nightmarish proportions. The discord caused a rift and through this rift Unesta could enter. He tried to break free of his visions. Tried and failed.

The sun was high when he next became conscious of the world around him. His limbs were weak and his hunger was great. When he tried to move, his muscles had grown stiff. He dragged himself to the edge of the stream to drink. The water cleansed him and made him feel whole.

Nearby fruit hung from a tree. He had not bade it to bear fruit but somehow it understood his need, for other trees surrounding it were bare of fruit and had only sweet-smelling flowers for decoration. He plucked a piece of fruit and ate it hungrily and then another and another. The visions, though, were not done with him for, as the sky turned pink and red with the setting sun, he was drawn down again. Fight them he could not.

These visions showed him forked pathways. Things that could be changed or ameliorated with preparation. Why did the evil pursue him? Why could not humans live out their lives in peace? Why was there anger, greed, hate and violence? He had no answer to this. His visions showed many things: battles, fighting. Wounding. Not murder, though.

His mind engaged, trying to perceive why this was so. *The oath prevented murder?* The vision continued and he dove deeper trying to understand, directing himself this way and that. Murder was the one thing that would break their oath. He panted as he realised this, his mighty heart thumping in his chest. Something that people did easily at times.

On and on time ran in his vision, perhaps for a thousand years or more, and he saw with pride that his blood mingled with all of those who dwelled upon the land. He saw with pride those who would follow after him. Then the scene changed and he beheld a vision of the land without magic—a sad, desolate place. It was the Ungiven Land and it must not be. It could not be!

It must be averted at all cost! This would be his life's challenge.

A vision came to him of a fortress in the mountains made with clear crystal like the finest glass. How could his people accomplish such a feat? How could he make this vision happen? For those gifted in using the *given* would study there and use that knowledge to help the land. Ideas and thoughts speared into him. He had to travel into the gate and find those who could help them. They needed more people, more livestock and more knowledge. His heart thumped at the thought of this. *What if he encountered her? What if she followed him back?* He tried to fight this vision, this dread knowledge, but it would not retreat. It was what he had to do.

Shabra shook him awake, frowning down at him. "What are you doing, lying about here while everyone else spends every moment working to scrape by?"

Vorn opened his eyes, struggled to focus. "How long?" he croaked out.

Shabra snarled, hate twisting his lips. "Everyone is frantic, thinking you have gone off to die or deserted them."

Vorn edged upward, his back to the tree trunk. "How long?"

"Ten days since you left. I have been looking for you for five."

"Ten days? Not. Possible."

Vorn tried to move but was so weak he could not quite manage it.

Shabra knelt beside him, his face softening. "I do not know how you came to be in this state. You do not look injured."

"Food. Water," Vorn rasped out.

Shabra brought him some fruit. Vorn ate. Ten days he had been languishing there caught in visions. After eating, he was able to struggle to the stream to drink. It seemed a waste of the *given* to call forth water where he had slept.

Shabra rested while Vorn composed himself. After eating some more fruit, he stood and walked around the clearing, feeling the strength once again return to his limbs. His clothes hung off him as he had lost weight. "I must continue to train and keep fit or I will lose my strength."

"You will have many who will wish to train with you." Shabra sat with his back resting against the tree. "What kept you out here?"

Vorn walked around him, studying the trees and sending his senses deep into the earth. "Visions."

"What?"

"I had visions of the future. Of what might be and what will be."

Shabra scoffed. "You are full of fancy since we arrived here."

"Not fancy. You have seen the *given* magic yourself. Used it."

Shabra nodded. "I have, yes, but I am not convinced." He plucked at some grass idly and stared at nothing in particular. "I feel it is some form of mass hallucination. Perhaps we are all dead and this is some kind of holding place for our souls."

Vorn sat down next to him. "Is there a difference? If we are dead then for our souls to survive we must follow our path."

Shabra turned to him, mouth open. He squinted then shut his mouth. "Are you playing with me?"

"No, I am taking what you said at face value and assessing it."

"Vorn...brother...we were warriors. What do we know about magic? About starting a colony or civilisation?" He tossed the blades of grass away. "Nothing."

"Yet, here we are using magic and starting a civilisation. I have seen how great we will become and how our blood will exist in our descendants."

Shabra studied him with dark eyes and shook his head. "I will never understand you. We will live for a bit and then die. Who will care about us and our stories?"

"Everyone," Vorn said with certainty. "What we do now matters much and it will matter to those who come after us."

Shabra snorted and pushed to his feet, shaking his head. "Will you come back with me now or do you wish to dwell here with your visions?"

Vorn looked around the clearing. "I will come back with you as there is much to do."

CHAPTER 5

The village they built thrived. Huts were sturdy enough to keep out rain. More-substantial dwellings were being planned to assist them to survive the winter. A storehouse was being designed to keep their root vegetables off the ground —dry and free from vermin. They had arrived in early spring but the chill and the rain convinced all that winter was sure to be colder still, perhaps with snow.

Vorn was helping with the gardens by tilling soil. He watched those around him and those carrying out other tasks. He heard laughter and saw a man and a woman talking. They had obviously formed a friendship, perhaps something more. It was time that people paired off. They needed children to live on after them to cement lives and build family and community. He would have to set the example. His eye caught N'Brell hard at work at her loom. She was a sweet-natured woman with a lively mind and was tall and elegant. He was not overly emotional about his choice. He knew, though, that he had to be sure of his choice and hers, for it was a binding one.

Around the fire that night he talked to the people. They all sat and listened, which was daunting to say the least. He had to be careful of everything he said. Shabra said one of his followers wrote down what he said on skins of the animals they had eaten. Vorn thought that he should write down his thoughts as well unless in some future time they were distorted.

"We must be bountiful in this land. We must take husbands and wives and make children so this land will grow. I beg you to take time to think things through, consider your personalities and wants and desires before pledging yourselves. For once you have made a promise to one another this cannot be broken. Understand. You will not be able to choose another. I tell you also that your joining will be fruitful for Argenterra is keen for children, for lives to fill it up."

"Are you saying that these young people must marry?" Faruni asked.

"I am saying that those who wish to partner up with another are free to do so. I ask only that they consider their oaths. Argenterra will bind them."

Faruni frowned. "So they cannot change their minds and marry another?"

Vorn studied the faces focussed on him. "I believe that this is the case. A promise is bound to be fulfilled in Argenterra."

"But how would that work? What is to stop someone from breaking their vow?"

Vorn lowered his brows. "We are yet to test this. My understanding is that the magic that we use, the *given*, will prevent us from breaking a promise. Although in time we will understand the nuances more."

Faruni nodded. "Praise the gods above that I am beyond such a calling." She looked to those around her. "You may marry and breed and I shall watch on from afar."

Vorn smiled at her light-hearted jest and kept what he could sense to himself. The next day he noticed the change. People approaching one another. Not all were traditional pairings that would lead to children. Most were, though.

They came to him first, though, seeking his blessing and assistance with the wording of their vows. His help he gave freely and very soon a common vow was made and the *given* bore witness to these pairings.

Shabra laughed at him from the sidelines. "I can't believe you, brother. Now you are starting a kid farm. How will we feed these children?"

"The same way we feed ourselves. You should find a mate. I recommend that you choose carefully."

"Phaw, what do you know? You have no mate. You can have any of your choosing and if you changed the wording of your oath you could have many."

Vorn shook his head. "Brother, have you no inkling of what folly you speak? More than one wife? How would I care for them and keep them happy? How would I ensure harmony in my household? Not only would it be unfair to them, it would rebound on me. No, I will take only one woman to wife…if she will have me."

"More fool you. You and your deep thinking and your analysis. I will wife whoever I will, whoever takes my fancy. Just watch me. I will have whatever woman I choose and will not be bound to one of them."

"Take heed, brother. Do not be so foolish!"

Shabra yelled at him. Called Vorn names. So loud was he that people stopped to stare and it was only the sight of Vorn, who remained calm, that stopped them from coming to his aid.

Shabra stormed off and Vorn watched him go with foreboding. Already a part of the vision was playing out and what he had done to prevent it had not worked. Shabra was about to make a very foolish choice.

N'Brell came up to him, shy and quiet. "Is everything all right?" she asked him.

He smiled at her. "Yes. I am well and my kinsman will do as he will."

She nodded and turned to walk back to her work.

"Wait," he said with a hand outstretched. "Will you not join me for a walk?"

She turned back, her long hair swaying around her waist. "I have some time to spare. One must take a break from the loom now and then."

He beckoned her to walk before him and he took her into the woods where he hoped they might have some privacy. He thought that she had a tender spot for him. He did not know if it was sufficient for a marriage bond. Yet, he would ask and made sure she had time to think on it.

They walked silently for some time. The woods were dotted with clearings that allowed the sun to coax forth flowers and in one such clearing they paused. Vorn, suddenly awkward, suggested they sit beneath a tree. N'Brell nodded and folded herself into a compact position and then reached forward to pluck a delightful white flower and sniff at it.

Vorn studied the downward slope of her neck and her head, finding himself short of words. She turned to him and her green eyes flashed with a smile. "Why are you so grave?" she asked. "Is this not a beautiful place? I cannot believe how hope fills my heart. It's like I breathe it in with each breath I take. I thought we were doomed. I thought I had lost the thread of happiness. I thought I would never feel joy again. Now, you have brought us here. To this Silverland. I will be forever grateful." She smiled, lowered her eyes and then threaded the flower into her hair.

Ah, he thought. A dilemma. *If I ask her to join with me she will do so out of gratitude.* He did not want that. He was young enough to want desire and love in his union. Now he had brought her here, he did not know what to say.

He was saved after a few moments by N'Brell speaking for herself. "You spoke last night about people pairing up."

Vorn's cheeks heated up and he prayed that his cheeks were not red for that would not do. "Yes. I can see our descendants making much of this place."

"And what of yourself?" she asked, lifting her gaze to his.

"Me?" he responding in a voice that choked off.

"Yes, you. Is there none among us who you could see yourself with in your elder years?"

He was definitely blushing. "Yes," he replied.

"Oh? I see…" She lowered her face and stared at her fingers, which twisted this way and that.

He reached out and took those hands in his. It was time he got some courage. Clearly it had been hard for her to speak up and the more he was around her the more he liked her, the more he felt kinship with her and the more he wanted her. Her head snapped up and her eyes widened at his touch. "It is you who I wish to be with if you will have me. I do not wish to pressure you…"

"Yes," she said. "Definitely yes. From the first moment you stood there head and shoulders above the rest. If the moment had not been fraught with danger I would have…"

He smiled. "You would have…?"

She blushed and turned her face away. "Do not ask me. It is embarrassing."

"Will you not sit closer to me?" he asked, heart beating erratically.

She nodded and stood up and then sat closer to him, close enough for their bodies to touch and for his arm to go around her. She nestled her head in the crook of his shoulder and he put his arm around her. They sat there for maybe an hour or more, just breathing, just getting used to each other. "Will you make a vow to me?" she asked quietly.

"Yes, if you will have me."

"We will have many fine children."

"That we will."

"We will go well together, I think. If you do not mind that I will speak up when I do not agree with things you say."

"I expect nothing less. I wish you to be who you are, not who you expect that I want. You are clever and talented and we will need all of your gifts."

She sighed and tilted up her face. "Will you kiss me?" she asked.

Vorn did willingly, savouring the taste of her for some time. "We will make our vows this night in front of the others."

"So soon?" she asked. "I have nothing fit to wear."

They both laughed at this. "Neither do I. For us to fulfil our vows we do not need clothes."

"Indeed, they would get in the way."

CHAPTER 6

UNBREAKABLE OATH

irelight flickered and burnished the clearing with a warm yellow glow. White flowers decorated N'Brell's hair and a simple robe enveloped her. A simple garment fashioned in a hurry by Faruni and other helpers. Vorn had gone to the stream to wash. It had been a cold and brisk bath, complete with chattering teeth and shivering flesh, but he had succeeded in cleaning himself. He had only a vest that was clean enough to wear. His shirt was long ago given up for rags. His breeches, too, had seen better days, but with some mending were decent. His hair, however, was washed and combed and it graced his shoulders. His scars had all healed and inside himself he sensed some spiritual healing as well. He welcomed this coming marriage. It was a new start for him, and N'Brell would make a

wonderful companion and her support would help
him in the tasks that lay ahead.

N'Brell looked up at him, a warm, sensuous glow
in her eyes. The bath had definitely been worth it.
They had kissed in the woods and he knew then that
they were a passionate match and that the making of
children would be no burden. He longed to hold her
against him and by the look in her eye, she felt the
same.

He took her hand in his and spoke his vow. "As
the *given* is my witness, I take thee, N'Brell, as my life
partner, wife and helpmate. I pledge to hold unto
you, to serve you in mind and in body. My vow is
true and unwavering. "

N'Brell repeated her vow. Vorn blinked for when
the words were spoken he sensed the oath take hold,
then it settled on him like skin.

Special food had been prepared for their celebra-
tion—a haunch of roast meat, roast toffel and
greens. More honey had been found and a dessert of
toffel had also been made. Vorn was a big man with
a big appetite so he enjoyed the food.

Shabra looked on the proceedings with his
habitual scowl. N'Brell talked to the women she
worked with so Vorn took a moment to speak to his
brother. "What ails you, Shab!" he said, using his
childhood pet name.

"Nothing. I'm looking at you making a fool of
yourself. You no more love that woman than you do

any other. What makes her so special? I thought you said we should consider carefully."

Vorn turned to gaze upon his wife. "I did consider well. If I appear foolish, it is only with desire and anticipation. N'Brell is easy to love. I wish you the same for your own union."

"You are a hypocrite. Just watch me." Shabra waved his hand. "I can have any of these women. I just have to lay my hand on one and they will be mine. Being your brother has some advantages."

Vorn drew back, surprised by the vitriol in these comments. "No. Do not do that, I beg you. I thought long before approaching N'Brell."

"How long was that…five minutes? You only made your holy pronouncement a day or so ago. Yet here you are making a vow."

"That does not mean I have not been thinking about it for longer."

But Shabra had walked away. Vorn frowned, worried at the outcome of this and trying to see the pathways in the future he had seen in his vision to the actions of now.

Later he saw Shabra with the people who had been in the pathway between worlds, people from a different culture. Shabra walked among them, chest thrust out like some kind of cock among the hens, trying to impress. It was like watching a collision in progress that he could not prevent.

He saw the woman first. Not a young woman, yet

beautiful all the same. Her eyes were blue and were stunning against the olive of her skin. Her hair was hidden by a colourful headcloth and she walked up to Shabra with confidence. It was Lilt.

Shabra saw her. "Here," he said, tugging on the woman's arm. "I take this one for wife."

Vorn stiffened, appalled at the affront given to the woman and her people. He was surprised however, when the woman bowed her head and thanked Shabra.

"I am Lilt, Lilt of the blue eyes. I will take you, fine sir, for husband."

Shabra was like a man drunk. He grabbed the woman to him and tried to maul her mouth with his. She expertly turned her face so that his mouth met her cheek. "Shall we speak our vows?"

With that she took Shabra's hand and led him to the fire where they could speak their oaths in front of witnesses. Not that they needed witnesses, because the land heard every promise. Wedding vows were shared because they built a sense of community. It was something they had done on Yulandir and it made sense to continue the practice in Argenterra.

N'Brell came up beside him and asked what was going on. She, too, looked appalled when he explained what had occurred. "Oh dear."

Vorn nodded, but he was not about to let his brother's choice affect his own. He leaned down to whisper in N'Brell's ear and she smiled and nodded. Hand in hand, they went to his hut and in the darkness they clung together, flesh against flesh. By morning, Vorn was certain that his first child was already growing within N'Brell and what a joyful joining it was. Many times they made love, giving to each other over and over again. He did not feel worthy of such joy, for guilt still clung to him, but he was able to push it aside long enough to enjoy N'Brell's gift.

Shabra was about the next morning as well. He had a smile on his face, but Vorn thought it was feigned. Unfortunately, he did not know if what he saw was what he wanted to see or what was actually there. Shabra irritated him in many ways. If anything, his brother had become surlier and angrier as each day passed and Vorn knew not what was causing it. Worse, he did not know how to fix it.

Could it be something as simple as jealousy? He would not credit that his half-brother would envy him this position—being responsible for so many, teaching them about magic that Vorn himself was only just coming to understand? Shabra barely believed in the *given* magic. Shabra was able to call water forth. Vorn had seen that with his own eyes. Yet when he had tried to engage his brother in conceptual discussions about the nature of the *given* magic, Shabra fobbed him off. Vorn considered himself alone in his perception and that was not an easy burden. What would happen if he died? How would his people fare?

He took his thoughts from Shabra, accepting that his brother's fate was his own. Vorn had more important worries.

Vorn went to work in the gardens, wondering at how fast the food grew. Surely the land was helping them as if it was sentient. That thought had him in need of solitude so he went to find N'Brell and let her know that he was off to the woods to meditate and not to worry if he was late.

"Take care, husband," she said.

"I will. See you soon," he replied with warmth in his heart. The way she said "husband" truly warmed him. A family was something he had never looked for and, now that he had one, he never wanted to lose it.

Before he entered the woods, he came across Shabra scowling as savagely has he had ever seen him. "What troubles you, brother?"

"As if you didn't know."

Vorn paused, taken aback. "Did your wedding night pass off well?"

Shabra moved quickly and punched him. Vorn reeled from the blow, taking a step or two back from the force of it. He rubbed at his jaw, perplexed. In their younger days, they had fought as brothers are wont to do but not so much now they were older.

Something was seriously upsetting his kinsman. "Why did you do that?"

"You know...oh you know..." His voice was a growl. "You forced me into it. Forced me to choose her."

"Lilt?"

"Yes," he almost spat at him. "That she-cat."

Vorn gazed longingly at the woods and the place where he could relax and contemplate but he could not walk away from his brother. Not now.

"What happened?" Vorn asked.

Shabra shook his head. "You will laugh at me."

"I promise I will not."

Shabra looked around and then urged Vorn further into the edge of the woods so none could overhear. "She rode me."

Vorn squinted. "Excuse me?"

"You know...she rode me. Took me in her way. She would not let me be the man."

Vorn considered this and wondered how it could be a bad thing for surely he had let N'Brell ride him as he had her. Yet, something in his relationship with Lilt had upset Shabra.

"Did you not have satisfaction?"

Shabra growled at him. "Are you trying to be an idiot? Of course I did not get satisfaction. You do not understand. She rode me, took from me and gave nothing in return."

Vorn could not picture this. "And this morning. Did you not join again with the morning's light?"

Vorn's mind was full of his joining and he could not hide his grin.

"No. I went off seeking the comfort of another." He jerked his head in the vicinity of the little village. "I had been enjoying her favours recently."

This surprised and yet did not surprise Vorn. His brother was none too careful in his dealings with people, particularly women. "And what happened?" Vorn asked but he was certain what the outcome had been.

"I could not. I could not get it up. I could not approach her. The girl tried but she could not either. It was as if there was a barrier between us."

Vorn tried to be sympathetic but his brother had been warned. "That is difficult. Did you care for this woman?"

"Don't be ridiculous. I care for no woman."

"And your wife?" Vorn asked.

"Phaw! She is not a wife but a bane on all men."

"Yet, you cannot lay with another."

"I am starting to believe that. Why did you not tell me? Now I am stuck with that...that..." He waved his hand in the direction of Lilt's part of the camp.

"I did tell you. I tried to warn you to choose with care. You would not listen."

Shabra yelled at him, tried to hit him again, and

Vorn grabbed his fists and threw him off. Shabra yelled into his face and stormed off. Vorn found the altercation disturbing. Not that Shabra could hurt him seriously. That would go against the vow, but Shabra could stir up discontent, dissent, disharmony.

Yet there was little he could do as Shabra's choice had been made and a vow sworn. He should visit Lilt and welcome her to the family. He would do what he could to help his brother.

A breeze shifted the branches about him and he rubbed his chin, easing the bruising from his brother's blow. It was time. He had much to think upon. He wanted to go so he could return again. He wanted the comfort of N'Brell's embrace and the smooth motions of their love making. It would not take all his troubles away but it would ease his soul.

Yet he turned away from the path to the woods. It was best not to put off his visit with his sister-in-law. He walked among the tents of Lilt's people. Some of the tents were made from blankets strung between trees. He noticed that none had huts. It must have been by choice. They had some supplies, too, so their flight had been better planned than his own. People stood as he walked into their part of the village. Dark eyes glittered as he walked past. He nodded to them, smiling, raising a hand in greeting. At the rear of this camp was a large tent. The flap moved and Lilt came out to greet him.

"Vorn," she said with a slight inclination of her head. "Welcome, brother."

She held open the tent flap and beckoned for him to enter. It was dark inside the tent and incense burned in the corner. Cushions littered the ground.

"Please take a seat," Lilt said as she seated herself.

Vorn sat on a cushion and realised it had been stuffed with dried grass. Very ingenious, he thought. "I came to pay my respects to you," Vorn said.

"Your presence is most gratifying. I am sure your brother choosing me for a wife was a surprise."

Vorn blinked. "Not for the reasons that you think. Were you not surprised by his..." He opened his hands. He could not say impulse for that would be insulting. "Choice?"

"Not at all. I understand your brother... perfectly."

"That is good then. I wish you a harmonious union."

Lilt burst out laughing. Vorn blinked and was not able to hide his surprise.

"You do not have to beat around the bush with me, Vorn. I am well aware of what your brother thinks of me. He is quite able to express himself and I am quite able to understand him. He seeks to dominate me and I'm afraid that I will not be dominated. I took him to husband, although he thinks he took me. I saw where the power lay—with you—but I also saw that your heart was engaged. That left your kinsman. I work to further the cause of my people. I would do anything to make sure they are treated fairly. The best way was through your brother."

Vorn frowned. "But why would you fear to be treated differently? Has someone acted wrongly toward you?"

Lilt smiled but there was nothing sweet about the expression. It was a smile of a mother who knew the truth of something when a child lied. "Our experience has been one of harassment and banishment. We fled our home because we risked death if we stayed. It is not the first time we have been thus treated. We are different. We do not change our ways. We seek to live our lives in peace. Yet, over and over again we have had to flee. We are the 'other'. The ones that people seek to blame for every wrong. Just because we are different and separate."

Vorn was much moved by this statement. It was not something unknown to him in his own culture on his own world. It was not until he had become a refugee himself that he understood what it was to be outcast and homeless. Argenterra had welcomed them, all of them. He wished that Lilt and her people understood that. Yet, he sensed there was more going on.

"I wish to assure you that this land welcomes you as we welcome you and as I welcome you to this family. It is good to see that you are not a victim of my brother's whim and that you wished to marry him. I look forward to calling you sister."

Lilt nodded, then hooded her eyelids so that he could not see into the brilliant blue depths of her eyes. "I carry within me a daughter."

Vorn nodded. "You see well then with the land's magic."

"Yes, I can see well. Not as well as you perhaps, but I know that your brother's seed has taken and that the child is female. This is a strange world you have brought us to, Vorn."

"Indeed. It has much potential."

"Yes, but for good or ill?"

"For good, I am sure. Will my brother be welcome in your tent?" Vorn asked, because he wanted to know. This woman had what she wanted. His brother did not. Not that Shabra really knew what he wanted, he knew only what he did not want.

"Of course. He is my husband and is welcomed by all my kin."

With that Vorn had to be satisfied. Although, not content with the outcome of the interview, he had to respect Lilt for knowing her own mind and acting for the good of her people. That Shabra had been manipulated he was sure about. However, if his brother had just paid heed to his choices he would not be lamenting them now. Shabra had a wife and it was she alone who could receive his amorous attentions. For good or ill that bond had been formed.

His duty done, Vorn was free to go and meditate on more serious concerns. He needed to discover whether the land had a will. The signs were there but he wanted to know, wanted a deep-down understanding of this world and its effects on his people. He could not rest, suspecting it could harm them. Shabra had proved a point that promises, vows and oaths could not be broken. Vorn no longer had to prove that.

The deeper Vorn penetrated into the forest, the quieter his thoughts became and the closer he found his mind to what he sensed of the land. He sat in a clearing and saw what it would look like in future. It would be dominated by a silver tree, the crystal tree. He himself would plant it. He would take a branch from the barren-looking tree on the mountain, Glassy Mountain, the name he would give it, and plant the cutting here. He would nourish it and it would exude power, it would anchor the *given*. That was his task.

He slowed his breathing as he tried to connect to the illusive essence he sensed. "Do you have a plan for us?" he asked. No answer came.

There was intelligence there, only it was not something he could easily understand. It was not conscious as he was conscious. Not self-directing as he was self-directing. Yet, it responded to him. He worried for this village, for the future of his people.

Much needed to be done to reach the future revealed to him.

"I will be king of this land," he said. He opened his eyes as the words fell from his lips. The leaves rustled. Clouds sped across the sky. Nearby he heard a bird singing like the tinkling of a bell.

"I vow," he began. "I will not rest until my people are established. I will work until the crystal tree is growing in this very spot, until there is a Glassy Mountain retreat up there in the mountains and a settlement here in the valley. I will not rest until I have anchored the *given* in the south and to the east. I will establish the borders of Argenterra."

He felt it then, the forging of the vow, strong and hard; it clamped on his chest and stole his breath. His limbs grew heavy and then he blacked out.

CHAPTER 7

THE PRICE

*H*air brushing against his cheek woke him. N'Brell was there, weeping and holding him to her breast as she rocked to and fro. "Vorn! Vorn!" she cried.

He struggled against her. "I am well. I am sorry to have worried you."

He squinted at the woods around him. The light had changed. Was it morning already? "How long?" he asked.

"A day and a night. It is morning again. I was worried. When I saw you lying there I thought the worst," she said and hugged him tightly to her.

When she released him, he breathed deeply. He felt different. He wasn't sure in what way but that oath he had made had changed him.

"I am sorry for your worry. I do not think you have anything to fear from the land. Accidents cannot be helped, I am sure, but my encounter with the *given* magic has not harmed me."

"But it has changed you. I can tell."

He narrowed his gaze. "In what way? Can you tell me?"

She leaned back from him, wiping at an errant tear tracking down her cheek. "It seems to me that you have an inner glow and also your skin is firmer, smoother." Her gaze continued to track down his body. "You are more solid somehow. Like a tree is solid." Her eyebrows drew together as her gaze sought his. "What have you done?"

Vorn climbed to his feet and dusted off his clothes. "I will tell you as we walk back. I am hungry all of a sudden."

Her arm snaked around his waist and he draped his across her shoulders as they headed back. He told her of his vow.

"What would be the outcome of this vow?" she asked him.

"Time will tell. I suspect it will mean that I will live until my vow is complete."

"You will see your descendants make these wondrous things that you foresaw in your visions?"

"I believe so."

"That is a heavy price to pay."

"Heavy? How so?"

"You will tire of it, I am sure. Those you love will be lost and gone."

Vorn stilled. She was right. He would outlive her and possibly their children. Maybe he would outlive even his grandchildren. He had not thought enough about the consequences of his vow. Now the promise was made and the *given* magic had worked its will, he was bound to see it through to the end. His vow had not been specific. He had identified a few specific happenings, but that last part had been rather vague. He would die eventually, but he knew not when. He would lose his N'Brell one day and live on alone without her. He blinked at the thought of that.

Perhaps she would take a vow to live as long as he? He shook his head. That was a frivolous desire. He could not ask it of her and nor could he predict the repercussions. He had made his vow and already the ramifications were far reaching. If he became the king then it would be a long time before a replacement could take the throne, unless he chose to relinquish it.

N'Brell was right about the loss of those he loved. How would he bear it? There was a higher purpose though. He would see things through. The land of Argenterra would know his hand and he would guide things. He had to agree that it was for the best. He could not leave things to chance, not after what had happened on Yulandir.

Guilt rushed up at him. He had no right to do this. He had caused so much grief. How did he know his vision was right and that he deserved to be in a position of power? When examining his own heart he thought his intentions were pure. When he had brought destruction down on his own people, he had not intended that at all. That did not pardon him. Not at all.

Filamon, one of the younger men, came running up to him when they returned to the village. He bowed his head and presented a leaf-wrapped bundle to Vorn.

Vorn stopped in his tracks and released his wife from his embrace. "Thank you, Filamon. What is this?"

"A gift for you, Lord Vorn."

Vorn bit his lip and then with a nod untied the wrapping. The leaves fell away, revealing a book. It was handmade with fine leather ties. The pages were finely scrapped and beaten skin. Inside was a feather with a finely-honed point. It was a journal. "Thank you." Vorn was deeply touched and the coincidence surprised him. He had just been thinking that he needed to write down what he had learned and what he had discerned and also record his visions. Perhaps then they would stop haunting him.

Filamon grinned in delight. "We also made you some ink. It is not easy as the wood does not burn."

"How did you make it?" Vorn asked.

"We soaked some leaves and the water turned brown. Then we boiled it until the liquid went dark.

Faruni says it will make a good dye for her cloth as well so we are working on other colours."

Vorn bowed to Filamon. "Thank you for a most considerate gift."

N'Brell took the book into her hands and caressed the leather cover. "It is lovingly crafted. I also have been busy making things."

They continued walking to their hut.

"And what is it that you have been making?"

"Why, a shirt for you. As much as I love looking at all that skin, a shirt might be useful to protect you from the weather."

"Indeed."

Once inside their hut, N'Brell got him to strip and she bathed him from head to toe, inspecting him for injury. Then she produced a large shirt. It was rough and a beige colour. "It's uncoloured. This is the colour of the thread we have made from the palms. Faruni has been working hard on thinking up ways to make finer cloth. She is a marvel. This was my first accomplishment. Wear it and think of me."

The shirt fit and he then took it off. N'Brell frowned. "Do you not like it?"

"I like it very well," he said and drew her into his arms and kissed the frown from her lips. "But I love you more and would like to wear you for a little while."

N'Brell blushed and smiled, lifting her face to receive his kiss. "I like that idea. But you cannot wear me like a shirt. That would not do. We can share skin for a while. Although I am sure that already I have a child in me." She frowned. "Most peculiar symptoms."

He kissed her lips and then the tip of her nose. "Indeed our son grows in you. Argenterra has many gifts and sharing my life with you is the best of them."

She leaned back and slapped his shoulder. "Flatterer."

"What?" he asked in mock surprise.

"Life is the most precious gift it has given us, followed closely by hope."

"Yes, that is so. Life and a future that we thought was lost."

*T*he End

~

*V*orn and the First Comers is the first in a collection of tales from Argenterra, penned by the renowned story teller Kushlan Silver-tongue. The Silverlands series is full of references to tales of Vorn and the First Comers and other tales from the inhabitants' forebears. If you like *Vorn and the First Comers*, check out the first book in the series, *Argenterra*. The first chapter of which follows.

ARGENTERRA

CHAPTER ONE: LOST

The low roof loomed over Sophy's head as she ducked to enter the next lot of tunnels beneath Castle Crioch. "God, it stinks in here."

"You're the one who wanted to go on a ghost tour. Stop complaining." Aria lifted her lantern and leant in closer to the stone wall, her nose wrinkling. "The quilts and flowers would have smelled nicer, but no, you had to do something more adventurous."

Sophy peered over Aria's shoulder to see what her best friend, now foster sister, was looking at. "You could've said no."

In the cracks between the stones, mortar had bubbled and oozed, leaving a rust-coloured trail of froth. Aria screwed up her face. "Gross. I can't believe I let you talk me into this. These old dungeons and tunnels are disgusting and creepy."

"I seem to recall that I have to suffer the quilts

and flowers once we get out of here. That was the deal, right?" Sophy said.

"Yes, and you're not getting out of it." Aria sent her a piercing glance clearly discernible in the gloom. "You owe me. I haven't recovered from that awful story of murder and ghosts the guide told us."

Ahead, the guide in question's voice echoed off the walls and the rest of the tour group were lost in the shadows. "Don't stress, it's only a tour," Sophy said, waving her hand to dispel the dank stench. "It'll be over soon." She shrugged. "They just make up the stories anyway. Besides, I'm here to protect you if anything really monstrous comes clumping towards us."

Aria scoffed and resumed walking. "You'll have to. My phone doesn't have a signal down here. I can't even call for help."

The hair on the back of Sophy's neck rose and she swung around. Something was there—a man-like shape in the darkness, with red, glowing eyes. Sucking in a breath, she blinked instinctively, but when she looked again there was nothing. Unsettled, she said nothing to Aria who was already creeped out.

In a few minutes they had caught up with the stragglers from the tour group. Brady, their tour guide, had a broad Scottish accent, rolling his 'r' and mumbling half the rest. Light from lanterns flickered and jerked as people moved. Sophy listened a bit harder as the story Brady related took a nasty turn. "An' the Laird returned to find the heads of all his loved ones hanging from the walls..."

Her gut twisted. Betrayal, murder, ghosts lamenting. Were people really that nasty? As she listened a bit longer, she decided they could be.

"How much longer?" Aria asked. "Mum and Jeff will be waiting for us." The tour rounded a corner.

Soph drew out her phone to check the clock display. "Another half an hour, I think. I'm sure Maralain and Jeff will figure out the tour is running late. Don't worry about it."

"I want to go back right now." Aria hissed the words in her ear with a decided edge of panic

"Now?" Sophy turned her astonished gaze to Aria. "But—"

Aria grabbed her upper arm and squeezed with fingers like claws. Aria's eyes were wide, her breaths coming in short pants. "I need to get out of here."

"Like now?"

The light from the lantern quavered in Aria's shaking hand. "Yes!" Aria's voice was hoarse and hard.

"I don't understand."

Aria's fingers dug harder into Sophy's bicep. "Oh god! I think I'm having a panic attack."

"What the? A panic attack?" Sophy gaped at Aria. "But the tour isn't that scary."

Aria covered her mouth, as if holding back a scream.

"I don't understand…why…" Sophy was cut off. The tour moved off again.

"Sophy, please, I'm being squeezed in half. I can't breathe." Aria sobbed. That hit Sophy right in the empathy spot.

"Okay. I'm sorry I didn't realise." Sophy cast around looking for an emergency exit. But this was an old Scottish castle and not an amusement park ride where they could hit an emergency stop button. The tour group had turned a corner. Sophy had a choice: race up there and get Brady to turn back, or they could reverse their steps and go back to the beginning. It would cause less embarrassment to Aria if they just found their own way back. She grabbed Aria's hand. "Come on, we'll head back to the start. We haven't come that far."

Aria kept a tight hold of Sophy's arm. "Thank you," she whimpered.

They turned the corner and walked for a few minutes. A deep groan enveloped them. Aria screamed, bending over and holding her stomach. The floor pitched and rolled. Sophy's heart thumped and her mind went white with terror. She barely kept on her feet. Dust rained down on them. "Quick! The doorway!"

Aria's breathing sounded like a bicycle pump but

she didn't move. Sophy snatched at her jacket and dragged her over. "Come on. Hurry up!"

The tremor continued. Aria let out a scream and looked ready to bolt away. "No, wait. Don't run," Sophy said as she fought to keep Aria in the doorway. Weren't doorways the best place during an earthquake?

Aria screamed, panic taking hold. "Noooooo."

Sophy's heart sounded like a heavy disco beat: boom tish, boom tish. She peeled Aria's fingers off the lantern and placed it on the floor. Screams still fled Aria's mouth, creeping Sophy out. "Stop it." Aria didn't listen so Sophy gave her one across the cheek. Aria stopped mid-screech and then cried into Sophy's shoulder.

The earthquake ended, but the ground didn't seem to stop moving. It was as if the foundations of Castle Crioch were reorganising themselves and the dull thuds reverberating under her feet meant the building may not have survived intact. Could the towers have fallen? They had survived the quake but weren't out of trouble. She gulped: there was a big pile of stone above their heads between them and safety.

Sophy couldn't believe their luck. Was Scotland prone to earthquakes? Not that she'd heard. And if it was, why didn't someone say so before they came down here into the bowels of this place? Sure it'd stood for hundreds of years, but if she had known it was seismically unstable she would have thought twice about it. Maybe.

She listened for voices, hoping to hear others from the tour or the guide. It was eerily quiet except for the sound of grit hissing as it fell, timbers creaking overhead and her heart beat.

Aria stiffened, her finger nails pinching Sophy's shoulders. "What's that?" The absolute dread in her voice chilled Sophy. Peeling Aria's fingers from her shoulder, she turned.

"What the hell?"

Before them was a tunnel, one that oozed moisture and smelled weird, like freshly mown grass. Aria grabbed onto the waist of Sophy's jeans. "Don't."

"Don't what?" she replied stepping forward. "It wasn't there before."

"Sophy—"

A glove of cold air enveloped them, snatched them up and dragged them into the tunnel. Sophy screamed and flailed about, her stomach dropping to her toes. Aria's voice was in her ears so she seized onto her and drew her close. They were freefalling. Was it possible to die of fright? Eyes slammed tight, her ears popped with the change in air pressure. She struggled to come to terms with what was happening, yet even in the centre of her fear her brain worked. They were travelling somewhere: how or why she didn't know.

Sophy clung tightly to Aria as wind howled in her ears and snatched her breath away. Her long hair whipped about trying to suffocate and strangle her at the same time. When she dared to open her eyes, nothing but a blur of indecipherable colours surrounded them. The silvery tunnel sucked them down its gullet and become a nothing: a no space, a place of wind and noise and disorientation.

A sudden shift in direction and their bodies dropped, gravity returning abruptly. A force pulled Aria from her grip, her scream falling rapidly away.

No time for panic. A blazing light stunned Sophy just before she thumped to the ground, winded. For a long, uncomfortable moment she couldn't breathe. She tugged at the strap of her shoulder bag wrapped around her neck. Then the world went dark.

Sophy came to. She must have blacked out, but for how long? A second, a minute, an hour? Pushing herself up on her hands, she tried to orient herself, relieved she still had her bag and her precious phone. The light was dim, not dark like the tunnels beneath Castle Crioch.

Wind crashed through dark-leaved trees filling the space around her. An early sun dispelled the shadows cast by their trunks. How did she not get snagged in the branches when she fell? Glancing up, she wasn't sure she had fallen. A sudden pain pierced her forehead. What had happened? She couldn't quite recollect the last few minutes of her life. They were on a ghost tour. Except now she was here. And here wasn't there. "Ohh?" she moaned. Everything hurt—her head, her face, her ears. There wasn't a part of her that didn't feel twisted and bent out of shape.

A shrill scream sounded over the sound of the wind in the trees. Her head jerked up. "Aria?"

Sophy lurched to her feet and staggered at the pain in her head. Aria's next scream impelled her forward; she had to find Aria, had to protect her.

Aria's screams allowed Sophy to gain her bearings. Aria was close by. Sophy's fingers clung to the bark of the nearest tree, but creaking branches made her push away quickly. She didn't want to be squashed if one fell. Around her, light flickered. Dark patches came and went in her peripheral vision. She thought someone was there yet, when she turned, there was no one. Before she reached the shelter of the surrounding woods, a strange wind rocked her, and it felt as if bits of her were ripped away.

"I must have hit my head," she said to herself. "I'm imagining things."

Stepping under a large tree, Sophy called out. "Aria? Aria."

No answer. Sophy kept walking. How had they had become separated? Short shrill screams pierced the wind. Sophy sped up.

Aria screamed again. Unhurt, opening her eyes proved too difficult. She was somewhere else. Felt it, knew it in her heart. It was in the air, in the ground and in the trees surrounding her. The taste of this place was on her tongue. She screamed again and then let her panic go.

As her heartbeat slowed, she drew in a breath of clear, sweet air. Instead of scrunching her eyes shut, she opened them. Living things around her exuded golden warmth. She saw life flowing through the trees; saw it in the water burbling in the stream beside her.

Calm, she told herself, be calm.

Crawling on hands and knees, she put her hands on the trunk of the nearest tree and felt the faint pulse of its life. Snatching her hand back, she curled herself into a ball and rocked back and forward. It couldn't be happening, it couldn't, she said like a litany to herself.

Sounds assaulted her ears, making her lift her head and hold her breath. Birds, insects, soft leaves fluttering on a light breeze, all made joyous, vibrant and over-whelming noise. She heard Sophy calling her name. What had happened? How had they ended up in this place, this beautiful place? She could barely remember what she was doing before finding herself here.

Sophy ducked under a low-lying branch and pushed through some undergrowth. With her ginger curls covering part of her face, Aria sat on the ground, next to a pool fed by a small stream. Relief rushed over her: thank goodness.

Sophy knelt next to her. "Are you hurt?"

Aria didn't respond and kept staring wide-eyed at her surroundings. Sophy's head pulsed with pain and her stomach twisted in knots. She leaned over to vomit on the ground. All she wanted to do was lie down and sleep until the weakness faded, yet some instinct made her resist the urge.

"Sophy?" Aria spoke at last. Sophy brushed the hair out of Aria's face, and quickly assessed her for injury. Aria was unharmed, not even a graze on her arm or a smear of dirt on her jeans. Her eyes though were still wide and staring.

"I am here. We're okay."

Aria's green gaze met hers, focusing finally. "We are not...not..."

"No. No. We're okay. We're fine."

Aria shook her head. "This place is different. I can see it, feel it. And look, my phone screen is completely blank. Nothing at all."

Sophy's brows cinched together. "I know something weird happened—"

"We are someplace else. I can feel life here, see it in the trees."

Sophy's mouth fell open. Aria spoke with such conviction that she became uneasy. She cast a glance around her, but all appeared to be normal. "No, we haven't. We're in Scotland—"

"The castle is not there."

Sophy shifted her head, trying to pinpoint the castle, the road, the village and couldn't. She couldn't explain what happened. They were in the tunnel on a ghost tour...She shook her head. Nothing. She couldn't remember. "Well, maybe we're lost." She noticed Aria assessing her. "What?"

"Your eyes...your eyes..." The hint of panic in Aria's voice sent fear crawling up Sophy's spine.

"What?" Sophy pressed her fingers around her eye socket, thinking it quite likely that her landing had caused a black eye.

"The colour has changed from dark blue to...to well...black. And your skin...so pale..."

"Right, I'm calling Maralain. She'll know what to do." Sophy pulled her phone out of her shoulder bag. The display was dead.

"It's not working, is it?" Aria asked.

Sophy shoved the phone back into her bag, with a sigh of resignation. "No. The battery must be dead, though it was fully charged before we went on the tour. Well, if somehow we...er...the castle is not there then there must be a road or a village or a police station around here."

"Do you really think so?" Aria's voice sounded calmer.

"Yes, of course I do." Even though Sophy was rattled by their experience, she needed to be strong for Aria. The sooner they found Maralain the better things would be.

"I doubt if you can walk anywhere," Aria commented her gaze fixed on Sophy's shaking hand and then pushed her hair behind her ears. "You're not well."

Dappled sunlight fell upon the nearby pond, revealing clear water and clean stones along the bottom.

"I think I'm okay. Some water might help." Sophy crawled over to the water's edge and splashed cold water over her face. Turning back to Aria, she asked, "Better?"

Her foster sister stood surveying the trees and the pond. Their gazes met and Aria nodded. Something in her expression led Sophy to believe that her looks had not improved.

They walked for a few hours with no sound of traffic or signs of people. Aria had not renewed her unnerving chatter about 'feeling or seeing life' in her surroundings, which allowed Sophy to file it away under hysteria in a moment of crisis. She tried not to let the complete absence of technology or human habitation unnerve her.

They entered a glade. In the centre, Sophy saw a beautiful, silver-barked tree. Sunlight reflected off its prism-like leaves and the air shimmered with colour, shifting and fading as the wind tugged lightly at the branches. Sophy's heart lurched as she tried to get her brain to understand what it was that she was seeing.

Aria gasped. "Look at that!"

"Yes, odd," she agreed. Her gaze roamed about the clearing, trying to put a frame of reference on what they were seeing and experiencing. "Is it real?"

"Beautiful…" Aria said in an awed whisper.

The crystal-clear, almost-silver leaves were vaguely oval shaped with protrusions that made them appear like small, solid stars. They looked as if they could fit into the palm of her hand. Was it a construction of some kind? Was it safe?

Aria reached out and touched one of the leaves.

"Don't!"

Too late. The leaves began to play music. The sound reverberated around the clearing, like little bells tinkling. The melody amplified as it bounced off the forest, flowing back upon itself, deepening the song with multi-layers of notes.

"Listen to that," Aria's expression was full of rapture.

Sophy tried to block out the discordant sound. Even with her ears covered, the nerve-twisting feeling managed to snake up through her jaw into her eyes. Glancing upwards, Sophy spotted two silver leaves floating ever so slowly down. They mesmerised her, fluttering and skipping before her eyes. She couldn't dodge out of their way. One landed on her chest, right below her collarbone. Disappearing through her clothes, it seared her skin. Pulling at the neck of her t-shirt, she tried to get rid of it, but she couldn't see it, only feel it delving into her flesh.

She tried to warn Aria, but pain overwhelmed her and a strange sense of dislocation coursed within her body. Falling backwards into scattered leaf mulch, she heard Aria say, just before she lost consciousness, "Do you hear that? Feel that? Delightful...magic."

Next thing she knew, Aria was leaning over her and shaking her by the shoulder. Sophy's mouth opened, guppy-like, but no sound came out.

"Wake up! Did you faint?" Aria asked, cradling one of the crystal leaves in her hand.

"I'm okay," Sophy finally managed to say in a croaky voice.

"That's good. You know, Sophy, this tree, it's not normal. Now I'm certain that—"

Sophy sat up and saw movement at the edge clearing. "Sssh"

"What is it?" Aria asked. "Do you hurt somewhere?"

"There's someone there." She pointed to the woods behind Aria.

Two archers crept out of the woods behind a man, who slowly approached them. He was young looking, maybe twenty-something, and wore coffee-coloured hose and a brown and green leather jerkin. Sophy was hoping that they were caught up in some kind of medieval re-enactment. Her gaze flicked to the tree, and she quickly squashed that train of thought.

"Lord." Aria gasped and absent-mindedly dropped her leaf.

"Run! Get away," Soph said, keeping the man in her line of sight.

"It's all right. He means us no harm."

"Are you nuts?" More archers, with arrows nocked, emerged from the cover of the trees. Their chance of escape evaporated.

Aria turned to her. "They glow with a golden light and mean us no harm."

"But they have arrows pointed at us." Sophy climbed to her feet and tried to position herself in front of Aria. Obviously, Aria was affected by their fall.

The stranger approached them, hands held out

from his sides. He was tanned and well built. Soph
could also see his clothing in more detail. The collar
of his white undershirt, embroidered and elegant,
kissed the edge of his clean-shaven, squarish chin. At
first he bowed from the waist, left hand sweeping
before him and then he looked quizzically at them
both. In a smooth and rich voice, he said, "Please
move away from the Crystal Tree."

Aria gaped. "I'm not getting that." She turned to
Sophy and raised her eyebrows.

Sophy had understood him and that made her
frown. "He said to move away from the tree."

Holding on to Sophy's arm, Aria took a step in
the direction the man indicated. Aria whispered,
"How can you understand him?"

"Don't know, but perhaps we should do as he
says before they decide to let those arrows fly."
Sophy took another step away from the tree,
bringing Aria with her. Angling her head over her
shoulder, she checked the position of the archers.
Arranged in a rough semi-circle, they had bland
expressions, but there was no mistaking the tension
in their hands as they held the arrows on the strings.

"What language is he speaking? It sounds famil-
iar, but I can't seem to grasp it," Aria said.

Frowning, the young man kept his gaze on Aria's
dropped leaf, glinting in the afternoon sun. He bent
to pick it up, took a long step in their direction and
placed it gently into Aria's hand. She didn't flinch or

edge away and appeared quite comfortable with the stranger getting close to her. The men surrounding them shared looks and murmured. Sophy couldn't quite catch what they were saying.

"The Crystal Tree has gifted you with a leaf, my lady," he said, his gaze lingering on Aria.

"This?" Aria said, holding the delicate crystal leaf. "It's very beautiful." She smiled, then looked over her shoulder at Sophy. "I can understand him now." She lifted the leaf. "I was right. It's magical."

"Sure it is. Why are they pointing arrows at us?" Sophy glowered at the man. When his gaze met hers, his mouth tensed. She tried to fix her hair by hooking the loose strands behind her ears and refrained from scratching her neck. It didn't seem to help.

"Forgive me," he began, facing Aria. "My name is Dellbright. The Crystal Tree Woods are in my care, and the tree itself is sacred to us. It does not give gifts lightly."

"We didn't harm the tree," Aria said, smiling shyly. "I think it sang to us."

He nodded. "We heard. We do not often meet travellers in these woods. Have you travelled far?"

Aria smiled at him again. "Yes...er we don't know, actually."

Sophy moved forward to stand by Aria, ignoring as best she could the six archers with arrows clenched against their bowstrings.

"This is…Sophy and I'm called Aria… Where are we exactly?"

"You are near my home, Valley Keep," he said.

"Do you have a phone? We need to make a call," Sophy asked.

"A phone?" He shook his head. "No. I do not…" He chewed his lower lip, then as if remembering himself, he said, "Forgive me for being so discourteous, but I must ask you to accompany me."

Sophy heard one of the men behind her whisper. "There are two of them…"

When she swung round to look at who was talking, she met blank expressions. Turning back, she saw Dellbright take a gold chain from around his neck. "Please let me," he said, holding out his hand for Aria's leaf. He deftly attached the leaf to the chain. "May I?" he asked and, after Aria's nod, placed the chain around her neck.

"Thank you," Aria said.

His eyes, full of suspicion, moved to Sophy's face. He didn't ask if she had a leaf. Then again, she didn't want to say what happened to hers. She scarce believed it had happened and didn't expect anyone else would either.

"The archers are here because of the Puri raiders. Do not be alarmed."

"Raiders?" Sophy repeated, feeling dizzy. "What are they?"

"Nothing to worry about, I assure you," he said as

they followed him out of the glade and into the forest. The archers disappeared into the surrounding trees. Soph could only see one or two of them at any time, their presence enough to prevent escape.

The party continued walking, for perhaps an hour, when Dellbright stopped.

"Would you like to rest? You appear tired."

"Yes," Sophy said as she dropped to the grass.

"Can I get you some water to drink?" Dellbright asked.

"Thank you," Aria said breathily. "Water would be great, wouldn't it?"

Sophy nodded. Dellbright stared at the ground and took a few steps to the left. He knelt down and spoke.

Sophy's eyebrows shot up, and she looked over to Aria, who smiled as if the goings on around her were perfectly natural. Curious, Sophy climbed to her feet and followed Aria to stand near where Dellbright knelt. Water bubbled up from the ground like a playground tap. What the hell?

Dellbright glanced up, eyes crinkled with a smile. "Come closer and drink. The water is fresh and sweet."

Aria knelt, leaned over and drank deeply. "That's delicious. Thank you."

Sophy leaned over, her lips tracking the water as it slid back into the ground. She pulled up short of the grass and frowned. Dellbright's mouth hung open, and his cheeks grew pink. "I do not understand. I have never seen it act this way before. Please, I will call it again."

And he did, but as soon as she drew closer, it fell away. Her proximity to the water was driving her crazy. The suspicious look Dellbright gave her didn't help. After three more tries, and Dellbright's increasingly sour expression, Aria asked if she could look in Sophy's shoulder bag. Aria took the cap off a deodorant spray and rinsed it before filling it and handing it to her.

Sophy drank deeply, having the cap refilled many times before quenching her thirst. The water receded into the ground, with only a small damp patch of earth to evidence its existence. Fixing her eyes on Dellbright, she asked, "How did you do that?"

"I asked and it was *given*."

"*Given*? What is *given*?" Aria asked.

Dellbright turned toward Aria. "You do not know of the *given*?" His gaze shifted between their blank faces. "Argenterra is famous for its *given*, bounty and craft."

Aria said. "Won't you tell us about them?"

Sophy sat down on the ground and groaned with her head in her hands. Argenterra! A bloody nutter! This was taking the whole ghost tour thing way too far.

"Are you all right?" Aria asked, squatting beside her.

She threw her head back and glared at them both. "I'm fine. What is wrong with you?"

Aria leaned back and replied, "I feel perfectly well." Then turning her attention back to Dellbright, she said, "Please, tell us."

"Very well. The water was *given*. Bounty is for taking and Craft is what we make with our hands."

Aria drew her curls behind her ears. "I'm not sure what you mean, are your clothes *given*, bounty or craft?"

He looked aghast. "My clothes are craft, of course, but of the very basic craft, I assure you." Gesturing to the trees, he stood up. "Fruit on the trees is bounty. It can be plucked. However, if it is not the season for fruit, the *given* will ripen it. Such is the way of a traveller who finds himself without sustenance. If he asks, Argenterra will give it to him."

He stopped for a moment as if thinking of a better way to explain. Then he walked to a bush that was full of green leaves and small closed buds. "The water was *given*, but it was there under the ground. I only asked it to come to the surface, thus not so difficult. This bush has the possibility of a flower." He spoke quietly to the bush and stroked it leaves. The bud grew and opened to a beautiful, green-petalled flower, which he handed to Aria.

When his eyes fell upon Sophy again, the smile in

them died. "Let us continue on," he said blandly and marched ahead, stopping to make sure Aria was following.

Sophy kept opening and closing her mouth. The land? Bounty? Was everyone but her crazy? She raced after them. Two archers flanked her, giving each other hand signals.

"So, Dellbright, are you some kind of magician?"

He turned back to her. "All who live in this land may ask and it will be *given*. Wait, I think I know what you are asking. Do you mean am I an adept?"

Sophy nodded, she thought that's what she meant.

"No, alas, I am not an adept. The adepts are recluses who study the mysteries of the land. They have spent many hundreds of years studying them, including the *given*."

He continued walking, eyes constantly straying to Aria. Sophy chewed her lips and tugged on her hair. There was too much to process, too much to deal with. Her heart beat a little faster, and she tried to quiet her anxiety, until a couple of archers leapt out of the trees and startled her.

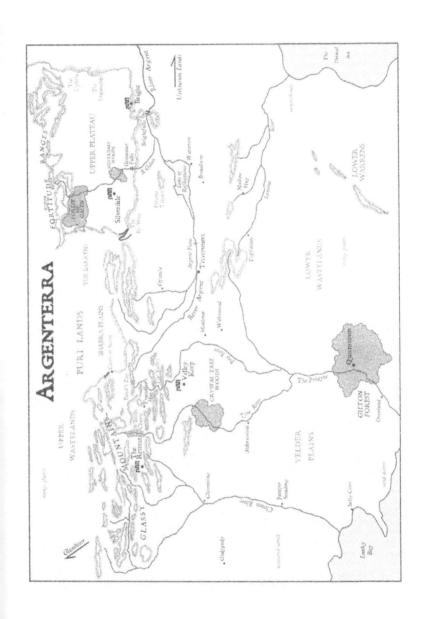

ABOUT THE AUTHOR

Donna Maree Hanson is a traditionally and independently published author of fantasy, science fiction and horror. She also writes paranormal romance under the pseudonym of Dani Kristoff. Her dark fantasy series (which some reviewers have called "grim dark"), Dragon Wine, was first published by Momentum Books (Pan Macmillan digital imprint) in 2014 as *Shatterwing*: Part One, and *Skywatcher*: Part Two. After Momentum Books closed down, Donna chose to publish the series herself. The whole series of six books is now published independently in digital and print-on-demand formats.

In April 2015, Donna was awarded the A. Bertram Chandler Award for "Outstanding Achievement in Australian Science Fiction" for her work in running science fiction conventions, publishing and broader SF community contributions. Donna also writes science fiction romance/space opera, with *Rayessa and the Space Pirates* and *Rae and Essa's Space Adventures* out with Escape Publishing. *Opi Battles the Space*

Pirates was published independently in 2017. In 2016, Donna commenced her PhD candidature at the University of Canberra researching feminism in popular romance.

Also available is her epic fantasy series, The Silverlands: *Argenterra*, *Oathbound* and *Ungiven Land*, which is a portal fantasy story. *Vorn and the First Comers* is a novella from the land of Argenterra published in 2019. The Cry Havoc series is a steampunk-themed fantasy with romantic elements, starting with *Ruby Heart* and *Emerald Fire*. It is based in Victorian England and features magicians and a very precocious Jemima Hardcastle. Another book, *Amber Rose*, is planned in the series.

Donna lives in Canberra with her partner and fellow writer Matthew Farrer and loves writing genre fiction.

You can contact Donna or find out more about what she is doing on her blog http://donnamareehanson.com

Or sign up to her newsletter, Wing Dust

Or on Twitter @DonnaMHanson and www.facebook.com/donnamareehanson

Short story collections

Beneath the Floating City: Short science fiction stories

Through These Eyes: Tales of Magic Realism and Fantasy

Robot Hearts (pending 2024)